Magic Ballerina
Holly and the Land of Sweets

Welcome to the world of Enchantia!

I have always loved to dance. The captivating music and wonderful stories of ballet are so inspiring. So come with me and let's follow Holly on her magical adventures in Enchantia, where the stories of dance will take you on a very special journey.

[signature]

p.s. Turn to the back to learn a special dance step from me...

Special thanks to
Ann Bryant and
Dynamo Limited

First published in Great Britain by HarperCollins *Children's Books* 2009
HarperCollins *Children's Books* is a division of HarperCollins *Publishers* Ltd,
77-85 Fulham Palace Road, Hammersmith, London W6 8JB

The HarperCollins website address is
www.harpercollins.co.uk

1

Text copyright © HarperCollins *Children's Books* 2009
Illustrations by Dynamo Limited
Illustrations copyright © HarperCollins *Children's Books* 2009

MAGIC BALLERINA™ and the 'Magic Ballerina' logo are
trademarks of HarperCollins Publishers Ltd.

ISBN-13 978 0 00 732324 1

Printed and bound in England by
Clays Ltd, St Ives plc

Mixed Sources
Product group from well-managed
forests and other controlled sources
www.fsc.org Cert no. SW-COC-1806
© 1996 Forest Stewardship Council

FSC is a non-profit international organisation established to promote the
responsible management of the world's forests. Products carrying the FSC
label are independently certified to assure consumers that they come
from forests that are managed to meet the social, economic and
ecological needs of present and future generations.

Find out more about HarperCollins and the environment at
www.harpercollins.co.uk/green

Magic Ballerina™
Holly and the Land of Sweets

Darcey Bussell

HarperCollins *Children's Books*

Contents

Prologue

*In the soft, pale light, the girl stood
with her head bent and her hands
held lightly in front of her.
There was a moment's silence and then
the first notes of the music began.
For as long as the girl could remember
music had seemed to tell her of
another world – a magical, exciting
world – that lay far, far away.
She always felt if she could just
close her eyes and lose herself,
then she would get there.
Maybe this time. As the music
swirled inside her, she swept
her arms above her head, rose on to
her toes and began to dance…*

Breaking the News

Holly's eyes widened as, slowly, she took in what her mum was saying. "You mean…"

"Yes," smiled her mum. "I'm giving up professional ballet!"

Holly couldn't believe her ears. She'd been living with her aunt and uncle during term time because her mum and dad, who were divorced, were away on tour with their ballet companies. Only now her mum was coming home for good! It was the best news she'd heard in ages.

"But won't you miss dancing?" Holly asked quickly, thinking how awful she'd feel if she couldn't go to her own ballet school, Madame Za-Za's.

Her mum looked thoughtful. "You know in your heart when the time is right to give something up, Holly." She paused and sighed, then broke into a smile. "Anyway, I'm not giving it up completely, I'm going to teach instead."

"Really? But that's brilliant!" said Holly.

"It certainly is," her mother smiled. "The only downside is that the ballet school I'm going to work at is a bit of a distance from here, so we'll be moving again. I'm sorry, love," she finished, seeing the look in Holly's eyes and giving her a quick hug. "I know you've settled in well here, and Auntie Maria and Uncle Ted have loved having you but, well, you'll have me as a teacher from now on!"

Holly nodded. She felt over the moon that her mum was going to be back, but it would mean she could no longer go to Madame Za-Za's ballet school. And that meant giving up all sorts of things – including her best friend, Chloe. She felt a lump in her throat, but smiled so her mum wouldn't realise she was sad. She didn't want Mum to think she was upset about her coming home, because she wasn't. She was really pleased.

"I'll just get my ballet bag, Mum. It's time for class."

On her way to Madame Za-Za's, Holly went over in her mind all the things that her mum had said and all the changes it would bring. And when she thought about leaving Chloe, her heart felt like lead. She hadn't exactly been good at making new friends when she'd first joined Madame Za-Za's, but Chloe had been so patient. It would be dreadful breaking the news to her. Why did everything have to change? If only they weren't moving so far away.

Still, there was one special, secret thing in Holly's life that definitely wouldn't have to change, no matter what – the beautiful pair of red ballet shoes that she owned.  She'd been given them by another girl when she'd arrived at the ballet school. She hadn't realised quite how special they were at first, but she'd soon found out.

When they glowed, they whisked her away to the magical land of Enchantia, where all the characters from the ballets live, and that's where Holly had met her friend, the White Cat. They'd already had all sorts of incredible adventures together.

A lovely surge of excitement at the memories made Holly leap up the steps to Madame Za-Za's two at a time.

At the top, she stopped and turned round. She and Chloe had started a new game of seeing how many steps they could jump down in one go, and it was tempting to have a go right now. But Holly knew that she was just trying to put off the moment when she had to tell Chloe her news. She sighed and pushed back the door.

The Saturday morning class was always
full, so the changing rooms were buzzing
with chatter as Holly sat down in a corner
with Chloe.

Holly kept glancing at her friend as she
got changed. She was trying to pluck up
the courage to tell her she was leaving.
But every time she thought she'd found
the right words, she imagined herself

saying them and then she saw Chloe's face falling. The thought of that was so unbearable, she couldn't bring herself to speak.

Then, as Holly put on her ballet shoes, another thought flitted across her mind, like the tiniest cloud passing the sun and blocking it out for a second. Maybe the shoes would be better off here with one of the girls at Madame Za-Za's, when Holly moved away. After all, they'd always belonged to someone at the ballet school. But Holly shook the thought out of her

head. She was just being silly. Of course they wouldn't have to stay behind. They'd been given to *her*, hadn't they?

As the girls from the last lesson came out of the studio, Holly's class formed a line in the corridor, with Chloe just in front of her. If only she could find the courage to speak. *Just say it!* she told herself sternly. *It'll be fine.*

"Chloe," she blurted out, before she had time to change her mind, "my mum is giving up dancing professionally and I'm going to live with her all the time from now on!"

"Hey, cool!" said Chloe, her face lighting up. "That's great news, Holly!"

"Yes," Holly went on, knowing she was

gabbling. "But the thing is… you see, um, well… we're moving away…"

There. She'd done it. She'd got the words out. "So I won't be coming here any more…" she finished.

"But… but…" Chloe looked shocked. "What do you mean? You're my best friend. You can't just go and leave me."

Holly hung her head, feeling her throat tighten. It was just as she'd imagined it. Chloe's eyes welled up with tears and she looked so sad. Then, without another word, she had rushed from the corridor. Holly felt terrible.

Changing Moods

Class was awful. Holly had been
expecting Chloe to be upset, but she was
quite the opposite. She kept smiling at
Holly, as though she was trying to make
up for her outburst earlier. But that didn't
cheer Holly up at all, because she could
tell that Chloe was only putting on a
brave face. Madame Za-Za was as patient

as ever, correcting their positions, describing to them the feelings they should have. She was such a good teacher, but even so, Holly could barely concentrate. All she could think about was Chloe.

Back in the changing rooms afterwards, Holly was desperate to talk to her friend properly, but she couldn't get a word in because Chloe just kept chattering away brightly, as though there was nothing the matter at all.

Right, now's my chance, thought Holly in relief as they went outside, but again it was no good. Chloe ran to the steps of the ballet school and took a big jump down from the sixth one, which neither of them had ever done before. Then she ran back

up and told Holly brightly that she was
going to try all eight steps.

"No!" said Holly
urgently, feeling her
heart race with worry.
Chloe was clearly being
reckless because she
was upset. "It's
dangerous, Chloe.
You mustn't…"

But it was too late. Holly gasped as
Chloe launched herself from the top step.

Then the next minute there were many
more gasps from other girls and parents
too, because Chloe had landed badly. Her
legs seemed to buckle under her and she
sank down to the ground, clutching her

ankle, her face screwed up in agony.
Without a second's hesitation, Holly ran
as fast as she could to get Madame Za-Za.

"Can we phone and see how Chloe is getting on at the hospital, now, Mum?" Holly asked for the tenth time as she and her mum helped Aunt Maria make lunch that afternoon.

"I've told you, love, Chloe's mum will be sure to phone us as soon as she can."

"Why don't you watch telly?" suggested Uncle Ted. "Take your mind off it."

Mum smiled. "Or what about your *Nutcracker* DVD?"

"OK." Holly's shoulders slumped as she put the DVD in the player.

Even the dancing couldn't take her mind off poor Chloe, and it was such a relief when the phone finally rang and Chloe's mum explained that Chloe had

broken her ankle and it was in a plaster cast.
Apparently, she was at home, feeling sorry
for herself, but had asked if Holly could
come and see her, and bring her ballet things.

"Oh, poor Chloe!" said Holly. "Please
say I'm allowed to see her, Mum!"

"All right, all right, let's go," said
Holly's mother, grabbing her car keys and
heading for the door with Holly already
pacing in front of her.

It could only have taken around ten
minutes to drive the short distance from
Aunt Maria's to Chloe's house, but it
seemed like an age to Holly.

Chloe looked a bit embarrassed when

Holly walked into the sitting room and found her on the sofa, her leg propped up in front of her.

"I was silly, wasn't I?" said Chloe straight away.

Holly didn't answer. She felt so sorry for Chloe and just wanted to make her feel better. "Can I draw on your plaster cast?" she asked, with a grin as she whipped three felt pens out of her ballet bag. "See, I've come prepared!"

Chloe giggled as Holly spent ages trying to draw a picture of the two of them in *arabesque* positions.

"It's a bit wobbly because the plaster's all uneven!" said Holly, flopping back on the settee.

Chloe sighed. "It'll be a while before I'll be doing any *arabesques*."

Holly bit her lip, seeing more tears in Chloe's eyes. "No it won't!" she declared, helping Chloe off the sofa. Then she held her friend's hands and gently encouraged her to raise the leg with the plaster. "See! You're doing it already!"

Chloe smiled bravely as she carefully
sat back down. Then after a pause, she
spoke quietly. "Can you… dance for me,
Holly? Please?"

Holly felt her throat hurting as she
changed into her red ballet shoes. She
didn't feel like dancing now. She was just
too emotional, and the sight of the magic
shoes brought back a niggle to her mind.
Something kept jabbing away at her,
telling her it was wrong to keep the shoes
when she was leaving Madame Za-Za's.
Still, she would block it out – at least for
the moment. She could never give up the
shoes. They were just too brilliant.

"What's the matter?" asked Chloe,
when Holly lifted her arms slowly, then

let them flop back down again.

"I… just need to go to the loo," Holly replied.

She didn't really, but thought that if she went out of the room for a moment she might be able to pull herself together. She'd hardly gone into the hallway, though, when she got a shock. The shoes were glowing. *Really* glowing. And a myriad of colours seemed to be swirling around Holly.

I'm on my way to Enchantia! she realised, her heart pounding with excitement. *Right now!*

Catastrophe!

Holly found herself set down in a world
of pink, just as though she was wearing
rose-tinted glasses.

I must be somewhere in Enchantia, she
thought, staring around at the amazing
scene. And yet it didn't look like
anywhere she'd been before.

She turned right round and gasped,
because a gigantic palace that looked like

it was made of white icing stood gleaming and tall against the bright blue sky. Holly pinched herself to check she wasn't dreaming. But she really was in Enchantia, because there was her friend, the White Cat, standing beside her.

"Oh, Cat, where are we?" She looked round in awe. "This is incredible!"

The White Cat chuckled and looked proud. "The Land of Sweets," he told her.

As Holly looked around her, she realised she could probably have worked that out for herself. There were mountains topped with whipped cream, flowers glazed with frosted syrup, fountains of sherbet, lollipop trees, candy-cane sticks of rock, jelly houses, fields of golden popcorn, even valleys of marshmallows.

"Oh, Cat! It's deliciously… amazing!"

"Not at the moment, it isn't," said the White Cat, suddenly looking downcast. "Come with me."

Holly was puzzled. She followed him down a sweeping drive of pink and white coconut flakes, into the palace. The grand reception hall was decorated with piped icing and Holly couldn't believe the magnificent ballroom that the White Cat was leading her into. Enormous pillars studded with multi-coloured fruit pastilles reached up to a caramel-coated ceiling. The floor was made of hard shiny toffee, the walls of Turkish delight.

But when Holly managed to drag her eyes away from all the splendour, she saw

that something was going wrong here. In the middle of the room there were groups of dancing Sweets, desperately trying to stay on their feet, but failing. White Chocolate Whirlers were dancing to Spanish music with clicking castanets, but they kept losing their balance and whirling off. Coffee dancers, dressed in wide silky trousers with little beaded tops and long flowing veils, were dancing to exotic Arabian music. Their veils had got all tangled up, though, and there was nothing graceful about the way they tried to pull apart from one another.

The Mandarin Mint Tea Men were trying to shuffle along in tiny steps to the quick high flute music of the Chinese Dance, but their steps had somehow turned into long strides and they kept bumping into each other. The Russian Toffee dancers, who had the fastest music of all, were attempting kicks and twirls and stamps and leaps, but they simply crashed into each other and fell over.

It was such a sad sight that Holly felt relieved when the music finally changed to a lilting waltz. Flower dancers got up from the edges of the ballroom and made their way to the centre. They were no better than the other dancers, though. Their petals had begun to drop off and were making the floor slippery, so they slid and skidded around, then fell to the ground.

Holly turned in horror to the White Cat and gasped. "Whatever is going on?"

"You may well ask." The White Cat took a deep breath. "The Land of Sweets is not just a wonderful place because of all the incredible Sweets who live here, but because the Sweets are the most amazing dancers too. Only they've got a problem. You see, the Sweets are controlled by the Sugar Plum Fairy. The trouble is, Sugar has been locked up by the Wicked Fairy in her castle, so the Sweets have totally lost their ability to dance."

Holly shuddered as a picture of the Wicked Fairy, with her hooked nose, long black cloak and iron grey hair, flashed through her mind. She had met her on other adventures in Enchantia and she was a very frightening character. Still, if

the Sweets were controlled by Sugar, there
was only one thing they could do. They'd
have to get her back.

Holly stood a little straighter and spoke
in a determined voice. "Come on then,
Cat, let's go and rescue her."

The White Cat's face lit up for a second,
as though he'd caught some of Holly's
determination. "Yes! We have to! Hang on
tight and I'll magick us to just outside the
Wicked Fairy's castle."

Holly nodded. It was important not to get inside the wicked characters' homes where their magic was most powerful. "We should be safe there."

"Let's not waste another second!" cried the White Cat, as he drew a circle with his tail in the coconut flakes.

Holly jumped inside and instantly felt herself being lifted up, then whisked away in a flash of pink and white coconut sparks.

The Wicked Fairy

Holly and the White Cat were set down
on a soft, springy lawn.

"Oh, my shimmering whiskers!" said
the White Cat, staring around. "Have I
brought us to the right place?"

Holly looked at the pointed turrets and
the jagged roof of the grey castle standing
before them and shivered. "Yes, it's

definitely the right place, Cat. But…" It was strange, the gardens looked different. The lawn was freshly mown, smooth and flat. "… the Wicked Fairy has certainly spruced things up, hasn't she?"

Together they took in the neat flower beds and finely mown grass. Then they both stiffened at the sound of a voice, *"One-and -a, two-and-a, three-and-a, four-and-a…"*

"It's her! It's the Wicked Fairy!" cried Holly. "Quick! Don't let her see us!"

The White Cat pointed out some stables close by, and he and Holly dived inside. They crouched down, hearts beating hard.

Holly put her eye to a little peephole in the wall of the stable. She gasped at what she saw. The Wicked Fairy had appeared

from behind a hedge and was stumbling along in a most peculiar way, her black cloak dragging behind her and her grey hair hanging down her back in rats' tails. As she moved along, she dipped down on every count and rose up on the words "and a".

   "What's she doing?" asked the White Cat, finding a little slit between the panels of wood and peering through it.

"You know, I think she's trying to dance!" breathed Holly in amazement. "She must have magicked up a new lawn, so she can dance outside." But then someone else came into view. "Who's that?"

"Oh, my glittering tail! It's Sugar!"

"You mean the Sugar Plum Fairy?" Holly's eyes widened at the sight of the beautiful fairy in her pink and lilac tutu. "But why would she be helping the Wicked Fairy?"

"How very strange! How extraordinary!" cried the White Cat.

"She's not locked up at all!"

Holly was confused. "So why can't she just magick herself away?"

"Perhaps the Wicked Fairy has put a spell on Sugar to keep her here," said the White Cat. "Yes, that must be it. Sugar would never stay otherwise…" But the White Cat stopped short as Holly put a hand on his arm to silence him.

"Look!" she pointed.

"Let's try a *plié*," came Sugar's soft lilting voice as the Wicked Fairy stopped her waltz steps and glared at Sugar, mumbling about how she was a useless teacher.

"First position," Sugar was saying patiently. "I… er… need to see your legs to check your placing."

Holly and the White Cat tried hard to stifle their giggles as the fairy raised her long skirt to reveal her thin, bony legs.

"Right, first you have to stand correctly," said Sugar a little shakily. "Rise up out of your ribs."

"Rise up out of my ribs!" came the scratchy voice of the Wicked Fairy. "What are you talking about, you stupid fairy? I'm not a contortionist!"

Sugar's voice faltered and Holly could see that she looked worried. "Er… I mean, stand up very straight…"

But the Wicked Fairy's knees were bent and turned inwards, and her feet were rolling badly as she clutched Sugar's hand

tightly, trying to keep her balance.

"Straight enough?" she asked Sugar,
grinning as though pleased with herself.

Sugar seemed to flinch as she answered,
"Very... er... good..."

47

And Holly couldn't help a loud giggle escaping. But she instantly regretted it and clapped a hand over her mouth, as the White Cat looked at her in alarm.

It was too late. The Wicked Fairy had clearly heard the sound, because her eyes were boring holes through the stable walls. Then she threw back her cloak and came storming across the lawn towards them.

There was no escape!

Prisoners

"Who's that? Who's there?" cried the
Wicked Fairy.

Holly and the White Cat shrunk back as
the door to the stables was blasted open
and the Wicked Fairy stomped inside.

"What are you doing in my stables?"
she yelled at them. "How dare you laugh
at me!" Her glinting eyes darted angrily

from Holly to the White Cat.

Holly stood, frozen with fear. *Oh no! What was the Wicked Fairy going to do to them?* But nothing happened. She simply turned on her heel, her black cloak throwing up a cloud of dust behind her. And with an ear-splitting thwack from the other side of the door, the bolt was slammed across. "I'll deal with you later!" came her parting screech.

"We're prisoners!" said Holly in a trembling voice. "And it's all my fault."

"Nonsense!" said the White Cat. "It's nobody's fault." He patted Holly's shoulder with his soft paw, but he was clearly as shaken up as she was. "Let's see what's going on now."

The two of them returned to their peepholes and for the next few minutes neither spoke, as they watched Sugar's attempts to teach the awkward Wicked Fairy to dance.

"It's impossible for poor Sugar," said Holly. "The Wicked Fairy is just too angular and angry."

"What's the point of these ridiculous positions?" the rasping voice rang out. "I want to *dance*, not stand like a flamingo or walk like a penguin. You're a useless teacher, that's the problem!"

"Let's move on to jumps, then," said Sugar, turning pale. "Try to point your toes and stretch your feet in the air…"

But the Wicked Fairy scarcely left the ground before she came down with a loud thud.

"That's it! I've had enough!" she yelled, pointing a long knotted finger at Sugar. "I need a better teacher. Be gone to the tower, you feeble fairy! Away with you!"

Holly and the White Cat watched in horror as Sugar disappeared into thin air and the Wicked Fairy let out a long cackle, before breaking into a chant…

"Whizz-a-whirl, twizz-a-twirl, coffee or tea.
A Sweet that can teach, now bring one to me!"

In an instant, one of the White Chocolate

Whirlers stood there before her.

"Stop staring, you dimwit, and get on with teaching me to dance!" commanded the Wicked Fairy.

But to Holly's horror, the poor Whirler, just whirled away and finished up flattened against a tree.

"How can she teach the Wicked Fairy when she's lost the ability to dance herself?" asked Holly in alarm.

"How indeed?" said the White Cat, wringing his tail. "The Sweets will never be able to dance as they used to, until Sugar is back in their kingdom visiting them with her special dancing powers."

"The poor thing," murmured Holly, as she and the White Cat watched the White Chocolate Whirler trying to get the Wicked Fairy to copy her pirouette.

It was no good. In seconds, she had whirled off crazily, and the Wicked Fairy was clearly furious.

"You're even worse than that feeble fairy!" she squawked. "Get back to where you came from!" And with a glint of her eye and a stab of her finger, the Whirler had vanished.

"Sherbet shazzam, bow down to my power.

I need the best teacher. Bring me a Flower!"

And to Holly and the White Cat's shock, there stood in the garden a beautiful deep pink Flower. Her shoulders drooped and she hung her head sadly as she stood before the Wicked Fairy.

"How can I learn to dance from this wilting waste of space!" mumbled the Wicked Fairy, shaking her head at the sight of the Flower. Then, her anger suddenly flared up and a ball of fire came shooting out of her fingertips, hurtling towards the frightened Flower. "Away with you!"

And in a flash, the Flower disappeared.
Holly could hardly believe her eyes as the
Wicked Fairy magicked one Sweet after
another into her garden, then shot balls of
fire at each of them, declaring them
"Useless!", "Pathetic!", "Clumsy" or
"Clodhopping", and banishing them back
to the Land of Sweets.

Her temper was growing worse and worse, and she was in a real frenzy by the time the last one had disappeared.

"Oh, my glimmering eyes, whatever will she do now?" murmured the White Cat. "Look! She's stomping off, leaving us trapped in here!"

"And what about Sugar?" said Holly fearfully as she realised the full horror of the situation. "If she stays imprisoned in the tower, no one in the Land of Sweets will ever be able to dance again! We can't let that happen, Cat! We've got to do something!"

"Quite so, quite so!" agreed the White Cat, his eyes darting this way and that, as though he was wracking his brain to think of something.

Holly looked around her, but she couldn't see anything either. Then she felt a little tingle from her feet, as if her red ballet shoes were trying to tell her something.

"I've got it!" Holly said. "Perhaps *I* could teach the Wicked Fairy how to dance!" And as soon as she'd spoken, she felt herself shrinking inside.

"Do you think you can?" the White Cat asked, the smallest note of hope in his voice.

Holly had absolutely no idea. But the Wicked Fairy was marching off to her castle and any second now she would be out of earshot. There was nothing for it. Holly took a deep breath and called out as loudly as she could, "I can teach you to dance. Try me!"

Last Chance

There was a stark, frozen silence as the Wicked Fairy stopped in her tracks, then slowly peered over her shoulder with a smirk on her face. Holly felt as though the words were hanging in the air, mocking her. *I can teach you to dance.*

Oh, what had she let herself in for?

The Wicked Fairy swung round and

started to make her way over more quietly
to the stables. Somehow this was scarier
than if she'd stomped her way across.
Holly swallowed, then jumped into the air
as the bolt was suddenly blasted and the
door flew open, banging against the wall.

"I don't believe you!" spat the Wicked
Fairy, pointing a sharp talon at her.

Holly knew she had to be brave and
stand up to the evil fairy. "But I..." she
began.

"Quiet, girl! You're only a human! What
do you know about dancing?" She turned
and looked calculatingly at the White Cat.
"Aha, but you might just do! You! You can
teach me to dance!"

She jerked her head at him and before

the White Cat had a chance to escape her clutches, she had grabbed him and was pulling him, protesting, outside. Immediately, the door crashed shut and the bolt was thrust across.

Holly put her eye to the peephole and watched her friend's desperate attempts to help the evil fairy to dance. He tried holding her hands, helping her to jump.

He tried to inspire her, by performing a
series of *grand jetés* around the lawn.

He even tried lifting her into the air, but
Holly could see he was struggling and
straining, until finally he let her drop.
This made her screech out in the worst
temper yet, as she blasted him back to the

stables, before slamming the door with one great whoosh of powerful magic.

Holly knew this was their only chance. She pushed open the door and ran out of the stables to face the Wicked Fairy head on. "I *can* teach you to dance. Look!"

She began the most complicated set of steps she knew, desperately hoping to impress the Wicked Fairy, but all she saw on the fairy's face was a sneer of contempt.

"Silly little girl!"

I must carry on. For Sugar. For the Land of Sweets, Holly told herself firmly, as she kept on dancing, trying to ignore the Wicked Fairy standing there with her arms folded.

"Just because you can dance, doesn't mean you can teach, girl!"

This time, Holly felt sure the words had been spoken less harshly, and took heart as she carried on dancing. Then a few seconds later, she definitely saw a look of curiosity flicker across the Wicked Fairy's face.

Holly began to plead with her. She had to convince the Wicked Fairy to let her help. "Oh, please, er, Madame Fairy, let

me have the honour of teaching you. I saw you through a little hole in the stable wall and I thought you were an exceptionally gifted dancer!"

The Wicked Fairy smoothed down her hair and a glimmer of a smile played around her lips. It was obvious she liked to be complimented, so Holly carried on.

"The trouble is, Madame Fairy, that you haven't found the right teacher yet. The Sweets weren't… on form… today. No, not at all! And it was definitely the White Cat's fault that he couldn't help you."

Holly crossed her fingers behind her back and hoped that the White Cat understood why she was having to pretend to be critical of him. "No, all you

need, Madame Fairy, is a special teacher.
And *I* am that person because I come from
a different land
altogether!"

The Wicked Fairy
stroked her pointed
chin and narrowed
her eyes. "Well, tell
me what you know
about teaching people to
dance then, girl!"

A picture of Madame Za-Za teaching
Holly's class flashed through her mind.
*What was it that made her such a wonderful
teacher?* Holly asked herself.

The answer came to her immediately,
and she spoke carefully. "Everyone has

the spirit of dance inside them. You just have to find it and bring it out."

She paused and looked straight into the eyes of the Wicked Fairy, then spoke in a gentle voice, forgetting for a moment where she was. "And I think I might be able to help you to do that."

Holly waited, her heart in her mouth, sensing that behind them in the stable the White Cat was also holding his breath. Would the Wicked Fairy give her the chance? Or would her plan fail completely?

The Secret of Dance

"All right, girl, teach me to dance then!"
The Wicked Fairy's eyes were boring into
Holly's, challenging her.

Holly swallowed. She knew she had to
get this right. The most important thing
was to help the fairy get rid of her anger
and calm her down, so she was in the
mood for dancing.

It seemed like an impossible task, but Holly didn't allow herself to hesitate. "The secret is to breathe slowly and deeply, Madame Fairy," she said.

"Don't be ridiculous, girl! What has breathing to do with dancing?"

"It's a magic ingredient!" Holly replied, trying to sound sure of herself. Just relax and close your eyes..."

"Hmm," said the Wicked Fairy, curling her lip. But she did as she was told, none the less.

"Now, slowly raise your arms to the sides," Holly went on. "Well done! You've got lovely soft wrists and elbows." It wasn't exactly true, but Holly was remembering how Madame Za-Za always gave plenty of encouragement, describing things so that her pupils knew exactly what she wanted. "That's right, take your arms all the way up."

It was actually working. The Wicked Fairy's face had lost its tight scowl. She was responding to Holly's praise and her arms were almost floating.

"Now let's try that again," said Holly, allowing herself to feel the tiniest bit of excitement at what was happening.

This time, the Wicked Fairy opened her

eyes, and Holly managed to smile at her. "You're really dancing now, Madame Fairy!"

"Am I?" The words were gruff with surprise, which Holly found strangely touching.

"And I was thinking… maybe, if you took off your heavy cloak? It might be weighing you down."

"Yes," said the fairy, frowning. "It's obviously hindering my progress." She flung it on to the hedge.

"Now, rise up on tiptoe this time as you raise your arms…" Holly continued.

The Wicked Fairy was rather wobbly, which gave Holly a moment of panic. It would be awful if she worked herself up into a temper again.

"That's lovely!" Holly quickly said, breaking into another smile. "It took me much longer than that to learn to balance."

Holly held her breath and got ready for fireworks, but nothing happened. The fairy just lifted her ribs and Holly couldn't help herself bursting into applause. "Bravo, Madame Fairy!" she cried.

And miraculously, the Wicked Fairy actually smiled at her. "Am I really... dancing?"

"Yes, you are!" replied Holly happily. "Take my hand and count with me, *one-and-a, two-and-a, three-and-a, four-and-a...*"

Together, Holly and the Wicked Fairy
danced round the garden, dipping on the
counts and rising up on the words "and
a". Holly couldn't explain it, but she felt a
real sense of pleasure in helping the
Wicked Fairy to dance. It was almost as

though through dancing together and sharing, Holly's own joy was increased. If only her friend, Chloe, could see her now.

Holly felt a pang in her heart at the thought of her friend. It would have been lovely to have shared this moment with her. Still, there wasn't time to think about that now as a sweet lilting voice came from the top of the high tower. Sugar!

"Bravo, Madame Fairy!" she called with genuine delight.

The Wicked Fairy tipped her head graciously and smiled up at Sugar, then suddenly stopped and picked up her wand from the foot of the hedge.

"Sugar Plum Fairy need stay there no more!
One-and-a, two-and-a, three-and-a, four!"

On the word 'four' there was a flash of gold and there, in front of Holly, stood the Sugar Plum Fairy.

"I've always wanted to dance and now I can," the Wicked Fairy announced importantly, "so you may return to the Land of Sweets. See yourselves out!"

Then she set off with her new found special waltz step, dipping and rising round the hedge and counting in a sing-song voice as she went.

The moment she was out of sight, the

White Cat came out of the stables and leaped across the lawn. "Let's go, before she changes her mind!" he said, drawing a circle on the fine lawn with his tail.

Sugar and Holly held hands and jumped inside the circle and, in an instant, they were surrounded by a ring of crackling, spinning sparkles.

"Home, sweet home!" said Sugar, sighing with contentment, as she, Holly and the White Cat were set down just outside the Icing Palace. Then she turned to Holly. "You were brilliant. You achieved the impossible! The Wicked Fairy seems quite a reformed character, now that she can dance!"

A bubble of happiness burst inside
Holly as she recalled the smile that the
Wicked Fairy had given her, when she'd
first realised she was actually dancing.
Her thoughts turned to her friend, Chloe,
again – if only she'd been able to share
Enchantia with her.

Chloe had been a really good friend to Holly and given her something very special in the way of friendship. Well, perhaps she *could* repay it. And there was only one way…

The White Cat began talking, snapping Holly out of her reverie.

"I do think Madame Fairy might have thanked you for your efforts!" he said, rubbing his head against her cheek.

It made Holly laugh. "She's obviously not *that* reformed!" she grinned.

Sugar stepped in. "Since she didn't,

Holly," said the fairy, "*I* will! Thank you! Now let's go inside. I think everyone at the palace should be ready!"

Holly and the White Cat exchanged a look of excitement, as Sugar led them across the grand ballroom towards two bright golden thrones. "You are the guests of honour at our Lollipop Carnival," she said quietly, as they took their places. Then she curtsied and flew off. "Let the dancing begin!"

There was a small silence, before Holly gasped at the entrance of a handsome prince. "That's the Nutcracker soldier who turned into a prince in the ballet!" she whispered to the White Cat.

He grinned. "It certainly is!"

Holly felt a bit silly. Of course her friend must have known that, living in Enchantia as he did.

The Prince and Sugar danced the lightest *pas de deux* together, full of lifts and twirls, then there were dances by the Mandarin Mint Tea Men, the White  Chocolate Whirlers, the Coffee dancers, the Russian Toffee dancers, the Flowers and many, many others. Everyone looked

so happy to be able to dance again and
Holly thought she'd never seen such an
amazing display.

"Your turn now!" said Sugar, leading
Holly and the White
Cat into the centre
of the dance
floor. And there
they danced
with each and
every Sweet,
and finished off
with their own
special dance
together.

"Thank you very much, Holly!" said the
White Cat, bowing low.

"It was a pleasure!" Holly said.
"I absolutely loved it!"

Everyone broke into
applause at that, and then
Holly felt the first slight
tingling in her feet. She
looked down. The shoes
were just starting to
glow.

"Oh, Cat, I am going to have to go in a
minute!"

She hugged her friend tightly, then
turned to Sugar. "Thank you so much for
the wonderful carnival!"

"Bye Holly. See you next time."

His words made Holly feel as if a
bucket of icy water had just been emptied

all over her. If she did what she was planning, then there wouldn't be a next time for her. *Think about Chloe*, she told herself. *Think about what an amazing time she will have when she comes here.*

Holly thought back to when she had first arrived at Madame Za-Za's, remembering how Chloe had insisted on trying to make friends with her, even when everyone else had given up and she knew she was doing the right thing. She wanted her friend to be happy.

She hesitated, wondering whether to say anything to the White Cat. No, she didn't want to upset him. Drawing on all her courage, she forced herself to smile. "Yes, goodbye White Cat," she said.

She blew him a kiss, turned a pirouette and felt herself being lifted into the air as the colours swirled faster and faster…

A Precious Gift

Holly blinked as she found herself back in the hallway at Chloe's, and realised that, as usual, no time at all had passed in the real world while she'd been in Enchantia.

A warm glow enfolded her as memories of the Sweets dancing flashed through her mind. Then she broke into a smile, recalling the way even the Wicked Fairy had managed to dance, once she was in the right mood, and how good it had been to share that moment.

Sharing... there it was again. Her mind was made up. She went back into the sitting room.

"That was quick!" Chloe said.

"Oh, I didn't need to go after all," Holly said with a small inward smile. She wondered just how Chloe would feel when she discovered the magic of Enchantia for herself. "Would you like me to do the *Dance of the Sugar Plum Fairy*, Chloe?" she asked.

Chloe nodded and got herself comfortable on the sofa, as though she was about to watch a DVD.

Holly thought of Sugar and the White Cat and the wonderful Land of Sweets, and danced with all her heart. At the end, she noticed Chloe's eyes were filled with tears, and that was the moment she knew

87

she was right about what she had decided
to do. Sitting down on the sofa, she slowly
and calmly began to take off her shoes.

"Chloe," she said, holding them out. "I
want you to have these shoes to remember
me by."

Chloe gasped and stared from the shoes
to Holly. "You can't give me these!" she
said, her eyes round. "I know how special

they are to you. I've seen the way you light up, every time you put them on!"

"Yes," said Holly softly. "They're very special. That's why I want you to have them."

The two friends exchanged a look and to Holly, it almost seemed like Chloe understood about the magic of the shoes, even though she couldn't possibly. Not yet.

She will one day, though, thought Holly, as the sound of her mum's softly spoken words came to her. *You know in your heart when the time is right to give something up.*

And Holly suddenly understood exactly what her mum had meant.

She handed her friend the precious

shoes. "Take care of them. Really good care."

And as Chloe took them, Holly felt a lump in her throat. But then she felt something glowing. It wasn't the shoes this time. The glow was in her heart, telling her that she'd done the right thing.

"Thank you," breathed Chloe.

"You're welcome," smiled Holly.

She jumped to her feet and spun round, barefoot. She didn't have the shoes any more, but she could still dance, and in her dreams, Enchantia would always be waiting.

Assemblés

This is the French word for 'assembled' and means to bring your feet together as you jump in the air.

°∘·*☆∘°∘·*☆∘°∘·*☆∘°∘·*·∘

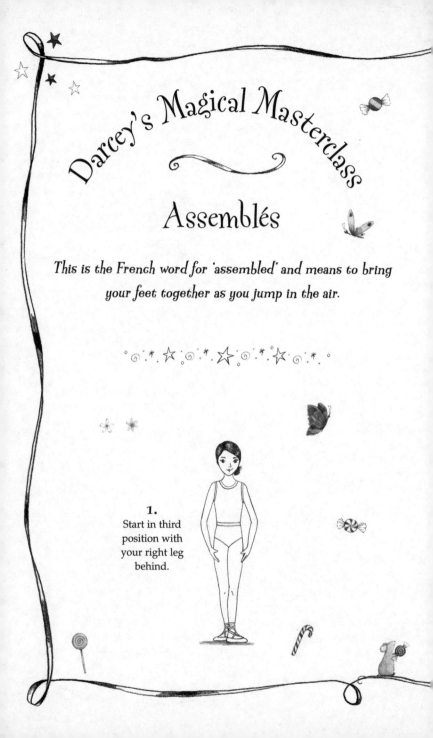

1.
Start in third position with your right leg behind.

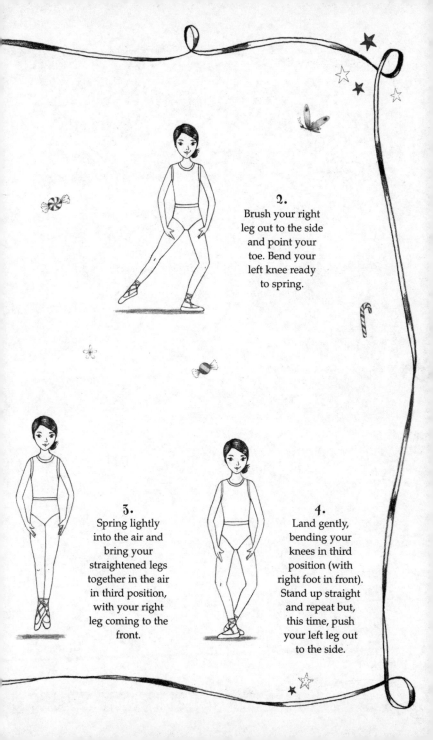

2.
Brush your right leg out to the side and point your toe. Bend your left knee ready to spring.

3.
Spring lightly into the air and bring your straightened legs together in the air in third position, with your right leg coming to the front.

4.
Land gently, bending your knees in third position (with right foot in front). Stand up straight and repeat but, this time, push your left leg out to the side.

Magic Ballerina

Read all of Holly's adventures!

Holly and the Dancing Cat — Darcey Bussell

Holly and the Silver Unicorn — Darcey Bussell

Holly and the Magic Tiara — Darcey Bussell

Holly and the Rose Garden — Darcey Bussell

Holly and the Ice Palace — Darcey Bussell

Holly and the Land of Sweets — Darcey Bussell